MAYBE IT'S A TIGER

Kathleen Hersom

illustrated by Niki Daly

MACMILLAN CHILDREN'S BOOKS

All rights reserved

ISBN 0 333 35166 5

First published 1981 by
MACMILLAN CHILDREN'S BOOKS
A division of Macmillan Publishers Limited
London and Basingstoke
Associated companies throughout the world

Picturemac edition published 1983

Reprinted 1985, 1986

Printed in Spain

To Tony, Helen,
Wendy, Matthew, and
little Joseph, with love.

We would like to thank Jane Fior for
all her help and encouragement, and
for introducing us to each other.
K.H. and N.D.

Alexander, and Beverley, and Junior, and Maria, and little Joseph were sitting on the hot dusty steps of the tall house. Beverley was minding the baby as usual.

They had finished looking at the animals in Joseph's picture book, and were wondering what to do next.

They could only think
of the games they'd played
yesterday, and they didn't
want to play them again
just yet.

"I know!" said Alexander.
"Let's play zoos! I'll go
fetch a tiger."

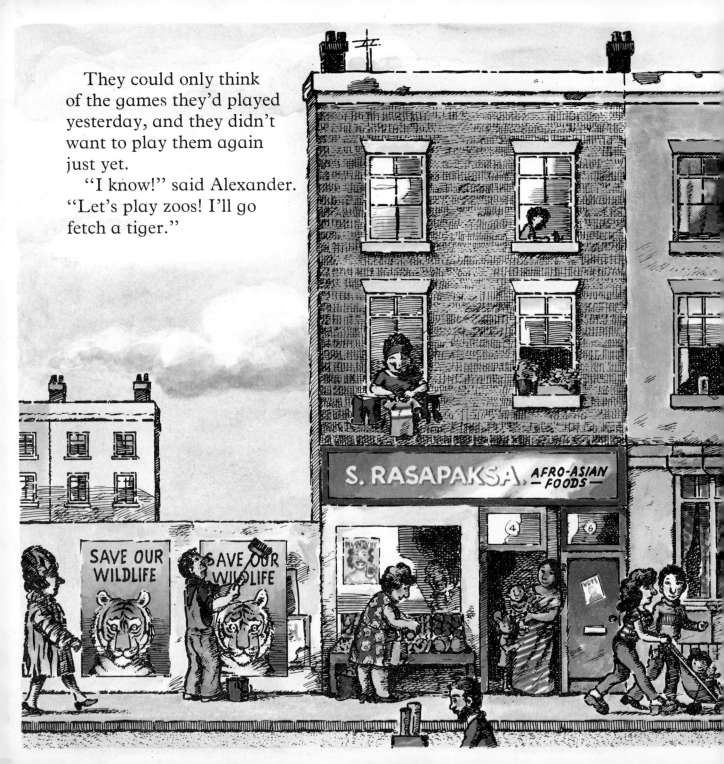

Alexander ran off inside, and up the stairs to the top
of the house, and came back with his tiger.

"That's no tiger!" said the others. "That's your
Granny's tabby cat!"

"It *is* a tiger," said Alexander. "Look at his stripes!
Just like the tiger in little Joseph's book."

"Maybe," said Joseph. "Maybe Alexander's tiger is *pretending* to be a tabby cat!"

"Maybe," said the others. And maybe it was.

"That's one!" said Alexander. "But a tiger by himself isn't a zoo."

"I know!" said Beverley. "I'll go fetch a brown bear."

Beverley ran inside, and came back with her brown bear.

"That's no brown bear!" said Alexander. "That's your new puppy!"

"It *is* a brown bear," said Beverley. "Look at his thick brown fur, and his black nose! Just like the brown bear in little Joseph's book."

"Maybe," said Joseph. "Maybe Beverley's brown bear is *pretending* to be a puppy."

"Maybe," said the others.
And maybe it was.

"That's two!" said Alexander. "But a tiger and a bear aren't a zoo."

"I know!" said Junior. "I'll go fetch a parrot."

Junior ran inside, and up to Mrs Mackenzie's room, and came down with his parrot, perched inside a glass case.

"That's no parrot!" said Alexander. "That's Mrs Mackenzie's stuffed budgie, and you won't half get a walloping when she finds out!"

"It *is* a parrot," said Junior. "Look at his beak and his claws! Just like the parrot in little Joseph's book."

"Maybe," said Joseph. "Maybe Junior's parrot is *pretending* to be a stuffed budgie."

"Maybe," said the others. And maybe it was.

"That's three!" said Alexander. "But a tiger, and a bear, and a parrot aren't a zoo."

"I know!" said Maria. "I'll go fetch a kangaroo."

Maria ran off to the house next door, and came back with her kangaroo.

"That's no kangaroo!" said Alexander. "That's your Alberto's gerbil!"

"It *is* a kangaroo!" said Maria. "Look at his long smooth tail, and his short front legs! Just like the kangaroo in little Joseph's book."

"Maybe," said Joseph. "Maybe Maria's kangaroo is *pretending* to be a gerbil."

"Maybe," said the others. And maybe it was.

"That's four!" said Alexander. "But a tiger, and a bear, and a parrot, and a kangaroo aren't a zoo."

Then they all looked hard at little Joseph, because he hadn't found anything for the zoo yet. But Joseph was very busy looking at the pictures in his book, all over again. At last he shut it up.

"I know!" he said. "I know where there's an ostrich, and a crocodile, and an octopus."

"That ought to make nearly enough for a real zoo," said Alexander.

So Joseph ran off down the street and round the corner till he came to the Pentecostal Church. Yesterday there had been a line of big birds on the church roof; birds with strong yellow legs.

There was only one bird on the roof today.
"Come here, ostrich!" shouted Joseph.
But the ostrich squawked and flew up
and away, over the roof-tops,
and down to the docks.
"Bother!" said Joseph.

Then Joseph ran off to the back of the bus depot where his Dad worked. He remembered finding a long hard scaly fellow hiding under a brick there, only yesterday.

Joseph whispered, "Where are you, crocodile?" but though he looked, and looked, and looked, the crocodile wasn't under the brick any more.

"BOTHER!" said Joseph.

Then Joseph ran back
home, and half-way up the
stairs to the big bathroom.
Yesterday morning he had
seen a huge eight-legger with a round
fat body exploring the wash basin.
But the bathroom door was locked,
because his mother was having a bath.

Joseph banged on the door.

"Let me in, Mum! . . . *Please!*"
he shouted, "I'm in a hurry!"

He ran to the basin but although he poked, and thumped, and shouted, "Come up, octopus!" the octopus stayed where it was. **"BOTHER!"** said Joseph.

So when Joseph came shuffling back to the others, on all fours, he was carrying nothing at all.

"Why have you been so long?" asked Alexander.

"Why didn't you fetch an ostrich?" said Beverley.

"How about the crocodile?" asked Junior.

"Where's that octopus?" said Maria.

"I've been a long time," said Joseph, "because I had to go so far. The ostrich flew away, and the crocodile has gone to live somewhere else, and the octopus didn't want to come. So I've brought an elephant instead."

"I can't see no elephant!" said Alexander.
"I can!" said Beverley.
"I can nearly see one," said Junior.
"Maybe," said Maria, "maybe this elephant is *pretending* to be little Joseph."
"Maybe," said the others.

Joseph said nothing at all. He just lifted his
trunk, and waved it from side to side.